To Charles, Eve and all the family – N.M.

To Daniel Archie with much love – A.B.x

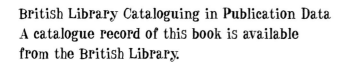

British Library Cataloguing in Publication Data
A catalogue record of this book is available
from the British Library.

ISBN 0 340 86603 9 (HB)
ISBN 0 340 87771 5 (PB)

Text copyright © Nicola Moon 2004
Illustrations copyright © Ailie Busby 2004

The right of Nicola Moon to be identified as the author
and Ailie Busby as the illustrator of this Work
has been asserted by them in accordance with the
Copyright, Designs and Patents Act 1988.

10 9 8 7 6 5 4 3 2 1

First published 2004
by Hodder Children's Books,
a division of Hodder Headline Limited,
338 Euston Road, London, NW1 3BH

Originated by Dot Gradations Ltd, UK
Printed in China

Slugs for Breakfast

NICOLA MOON AILIE BUSBY

Hodder
Children's
Books

A division of Hodder Headline Limited

The **WORST** thing about being

The **best** thing
about being a kangaroo is...

...having a handy pocket to carry all

your things.

The **WORST** thing about being a frog is...

The **best** thing about being a frog is...

...being able to swim without armbands.

The **worst** thing about being a hippo is...

The **best** thing about being a hippo is...

The **WORST** thing about being a snake is...

...not being able to play football.

The **best** thing about being a snake is...

The **worst** thing
about being an elephant is...

...never having a big enough handkerchief.

The **best** thing about being an elephant is...

...always winning in a water fight.

The **worst** thing
about being a tortoise is...

The **best** thing about being a tortoise is...

...having the best place to hide.

But whatever
you are...

...the best thing is always

The end.

may 28/11 pg 9-13 glued in it